Androcles and the Lion

and other stories

Miles
KeLLY

First published in 2011 by Miles Kelly Publishing Ltd
Harding's Barn, Bardfield End Green, Thaxted, Essex, CM6 3PX, UK

Copyright © Miles Kelly Publishing Ltd 2011

This edition printed 2013

2 4 6 8 10 9 7 5 3

Publishing Director Belinda Gallagher

Creative Director Jo Cowan

Editor Amanda Askew

Senior Designer Joe Jones

Designer Kayleigh Allen

Production Manager Elizabeth Collins

Reprographics Anthony Cambray, Stephan Davis, Jennifer Hunt

Assets Lorraine King

ISBN 978-1-84810-438-9

Printed in China

British Library Cataloguing-in-Publication Data
A catalogue record for this book is available from the British Library

ACKNOWLEDGEMENTS
Artworks are from the Miles Kelly Artwork Bank

Made with paper from a sustainable forest

www.mileskelly.net
info@mileskelly.net
www.factsforprojects.com

Contents

Hop-Toads and Pearls

A retelling from the original tale by Charles Perrault

Go and fetch the water!" yelled the widow at her younger daughter. "You can finish that sweeping later! And hurry back with it. You've still got to light the fire and peel the potatoes."

The poor girl hurried to rest her broom in the corner and wipe her dusty hands on her tattered apron. She never grumbled about being treated like a slave because she was good and kind and couldn't think badly about anybody. But how she

wished that her mother and her sister might help her out with all the housework now and again...

As the exhausted girl stumbled out to the well with the bucket, the widow's elder daughter looked up from her comfy chair and smirked. Fanchon was like her mother in every way: how she looked (very ugly), how she spoke (sharp and nasty) and how she acted (selfish and lazy). This was the reason why her mother adored her so: whenever she looked at Fanchon, she saw herself.

The widow's younger daughter reached the well and heaved up a heavy, full bucket. Suddenly, she noticed that an old beggar-woman had joined her. The toothless crone wheezed, "My dear, I'm hoarse with thirst. Could you spare me a little drink?"

"Of course," the girl said, and hurried to unhook the dripping bucket and help the beggar-woman to a ladleful.

Little did the younger daughter know that the hag who stood in front of her was actually a powerful fairy, who had disguised herself to put the girl to the test. The younger daughter kindly helped the beggar-woman to another ladleful of water and chatted politely to her for a while, before hauling the bucket back home.

How the girl's mother and her sister yelled and screamed and swore at her for taking so long at the well! "I do beg your pardon," the poor girl apologised. "I will be quicker next time."

To everyone's surprise, a shining white pearl dropped from her lips with every word.

The stunned widow woman picked up a pearl from the floor, bit it hard between her teeth, and held it up to the light to examine it.

"They're real!" she exclaimed, with a greedy twinkle in her eye. "What on earth happened at the well this evening? Tell me everything, or I'll lock you in the coal cellar all weekend."

The younger daughter was just as amazed as her mother and sister, and truthfully told them that she had done nothing but give a drink to a woman she'd met at the well. Pearls continued to drop from her lips as she spoke, and as fast as they fell, the widow scooped them up greedily into her pockets.

"Did you hear that, Fanchon?" she screeched. "Get yourself down to that well immediately!"

"Get lost!" the rude girl snorted. "I'm not fetching and carrying like a slave for anything!"

"I said GO!" the widow roared, cuffing the horrified Fanchon round the head. "Find that woman and give her a drink, whether she wants

one or not! We're going to be rich, rich, rich!"

Fanchon sulked and pouted, grumbled and cursed with every step that she lugged the splintery bucket – and it was only fear of her mother's temper that made her do it at all. She flung the bucket angrily into the well and moaned and groaned to herself with every wind as she pulled it back up. No sooner had she finished, than she noticed she had been joined by an elegant young woman dressed in fine robes. (It was the fairy, disguised as a princess.) "Good evening," the princess said politely, "would you be so good as to allow me a drink?"

"Oh, it's you, is it?" Fanchon sneered. "You're the reason I've got splinters in my hands, splashes all over my dress, and my arms are killing me. You'd better make it worth my while and give

me diamonds instead of pearls, that's all I can say." With that, Fanchon angrily flung the wooden ladle at the princess and dumped the bucket at her feet. "Go on then," she snapped.

No sooner had the princess taken one sip than Fanchon snatched the ladle back and humped the bucket back to the house. "There!" she yelled at her mother. "Happy now?" To everyone's horror, three great hop-toads leapt from her lips and sprang across the floor, croaking. Fanchon clapped her hands over her mouth in alarm.

"Whatever's happened?" cried the widow. "Where are the pearls?"

"I don't know!" wailed Fanchon, and three more hop-toads bounced, bulging-eyed, from her mouth. She began to scream and stamp her feet.

"This is all your fault, you ungrateful wretch!" the widow yelled at her younger daughter. She shoved the girl outside and slammed the door in her face. The poor younger daughter wandered off into the forest, sobbing.

The girl would almost certainly have got lost in the woods forever if the prince hadn't spotted her on his way back from a hunting trip. The prince was fascinated by the pearls that fell from her mouth, but he was even more charmed by the forgiving, kind way in which she spoke of her obviously horrible family. He took the lovely girl back to his palace at once, and after she had got to know and love him, he married her.

As for the nasty elder daughter, even her own mother tired of her moaning. The widow threw the girl out, and they both lived the rest of their lives with only their miserable selves for company.

Liam and the Fairy Cattle

An Irish legend

Liam and his mother lived by the sea. They had a small white cottage with a pile of peat for the fire outside, and a row of potatoes to eat with the fish that Liam would catch. They had two cows, and Liam's mother would make butter and cheese from their milk. She baked bread and gathered sweet heather honey from the hives at the bottom of the meadow. They did not have much in life, but they were happy.

But then there came a time when ill luck fell on the small white cottage. First the two cows died, one after the other, and there was no cheese to eat. Then the shoals of fish swam far out to sea and Liam would come home empty-handed. The potatoes rotted in the ground, and Liam and his mother were hungry all the time.

One day when Liam was wandering along the shoreline he came across two boys throwing stones at a seal. He chased the boys away, but when he went to see if the seal needed help it turned its head once and looked deep into his eyes then slipped away into the sea. As it dived into the waves he saw blood on its head.

Three days later when Liam and his mother were sitting by the fire in the evening there came a knock at the door. There on the doorstep stood an old, old man leaning on a staff. His clothes looked

wet through and he had a large cut on his forehead, but his eyes were gentle.

"I am very weary, might I come in and warm myself at your fire?" the old man asked.

Liam opened the door wide, and bid the old man come in. His mother pulled up a stool close to the fire, and warmed up the last of the soup in the pot while she bathed the wound on his head. He thanked her kindly, smiling at Liam, and Liam had the strangest feeling he had looked into those deep brown eyes before. But he

made up the fire for the night and they all slept peacefully until the day.

The old man looked better for his night's shelter, and as he rose to leave he spoke to Liam's mother.

"I have no money to offer you but I would like to thank you for your shelter and food, and I would like to repay the boy here for his kindness," and he turned and looked at Liam with his gentle brown eyes. "I know you have lost your cows so I will tell you where you can find some special cows who will give you milk such as you have never tasted before. Tonight is a full moon and the sea-folk will bring their cattle up out of the sea to graze on the green grass that grows just beyond the shoreline."

Liam's mother laughed. "I have often heard tales of these marvellous cattle, but in all the years I have lived here I have never seen a fairy cow."

"That is because your eyes have not been

opened by a touch with the heather that grows on the grave of Fionn who died all those years ago," said the old man and there in his hand he held out a sprig of heather. "Will you let me touch your eyes, and the boy's too? Then you shall see."

Well, Liam's mother felt she had nothing to fear from this kindly old man and so both she and Liam let him touch their eyes with the heather.

"Now," he said, "you must gather seven handfuls of earth from the churchyard, and then tonight go to the meadow just beyond the shoreline. There you will see the fairy cattle. Choose the seven you like the best and throw the earth onto each one. They will all run back to the sea, save the seven that you have chosen. Bring those seven back home and look after them in your kindly way and they will be with you always. Now I must return from whence I came. Liam, will you

walk with me to the sea?" and the old man looked at Liam with those gentle eyes once again.

So Liam and the strange old man walked to the shoreline. One moment they were together on the sand, the next Liam was alone. But when he looked out to sea, there was a seal, looking at him. Then with a ripple, it was gone under the waves.

That night, Liam and his mother did as the old man had bid. They gathered the earth from the churchyard and made their way quietly down to the meadow. There indeed was the herd of fairy cattle. They were small, no bigger than a sheepdog, and all colours. Liam and his mother choose three black, three white and a brindled one, and Liam crept up behind them and threw the earth onto their backs. The

rest of the herd scattered back down to the shore and ran into the waves where they quickly disappeared. But the seven in the meadow stood quietly and showed no fear as Liam and his mother led them home.

From that day on, Liam and his mother had a plentiful supply of creamy milk. The little fairy cattle would low gently in the byre and were well content with their life on land. But Liam would never let them out to graze when there was a full moon in case the sea-folk came to get them back.

Androcles and the Lion

A retelling from the Fables of Phaedrus

Many thousands of years ago there lived a poor slave called Androcles. Life was very miserable for slaves. They barely had enough to eat, and if they didn't work hard enough they were sent to Rome to be thrown to the lions.

One day, Androcles had a chance to escape. He ran and ran, until he was utterly exhausted. Then he crawled into a forest to hide until he regained his strength. He was just settling down to sleep

18

when a great lion hobbled out from behind a tree. At first, Androcles was petrified, but he soon realized the lion was not about to jump on him, but was holding out his paw helplessly. Androcles stepped cautiously towards the lion. The paw was all swollen and bleeding, and when Androcles looked closely he could see a huge thorn stuck in-between the claws.

Androcles pulled the thorn out, and cleaned the wound before wrapping it in leaves to keep it dry. The lion licked Androcles with his rough tongue and then lay down beside him and went to sleep. He kept Androcles warm all night. In the morning the lion slipped away very early and Androcles continued on his way.

Good Deeds

Years passed. But one day Androcles' luck ran out and he was captured and sent into the arena to fight. The trapdoor was opened and a huge lion came bounding up to Androcles. He closed his eyes, waiting for death. But then he felt a rough tongue licking his face. It was his lion! The crowds cheered, and the emperor made Androcles tell the story of the thorn in the lion's paw. The emperor decided to free Androcles and the lion.

Androcles kept the lion's paws free of thorns, while the lion kept Androcles warm at night, and so they both lived to a very ripe old age together.

The Lion and the Mouse

A retelling from Aesop's Fables

The lion was very hungry. As he padded through the tall grass, something rustled by his feet. He reached out a great paw, and there was a squeak. He had caught a tiny mouse by the tail.

"Oh please let me go, dear lion," cried the tiny mouse. "I should be no more than a single mouthful for you. And I promise I will be able to help you some day."

The lion roared with laughter. The thought of a

tiny mouse being able to help such a huge creature as himself amused him so much that he did let the mouse go.

"He would not have made much of a meal anyway," smiled the lion.

The mouse scuttled away, calling out to the lion, "I shall not forget my promise!"

Many days and nights later the lion was padding through the grass again when he fell into a deep pit. A net was flung over him, and he lay there helpless, caught by some hunters. He twisted and turned but he could not free himself. The hunters just laughed at his struggles and went off to fetch a cart to carry the great lion back to their village.

The Lion and the Mouse

As he lay there, the lion heard a tiny voice.

"I promised I'd be able to help you one day."

It was the tiny mouse! And straight away he began to gnaw through the rope that held the lion fast. He gnawed and chewed, and chewed and gnawed, and eventually he chewed and gnawed right through the rope and the lion was free. With a great bound, he leapt out of the pit and then reached back, very gently, to lift the tiny mouse out too.

"I shall never forget you, mouse. Thank you for remembering your promise and saving me," purred the great lion.

So the tiny mouse was able to help the great lion. One good turn deserves another, you see?

Whippety Stourie

Anon

There was once a gentleman that lived in a very grand house, and he married a young lady who had been delicately brought up. In her husband's house she found everything that was fine — fine tables and chairs, fine looking-glasses, and fine curtains, but then her husband expected her to be able to spin twelve balls of thread every day, besides attending to her house, and, to tell the truth, the lady could not spin a bit. This made her

husband cross with her, and, before a month had passed, she found herself very unhappy.

One day the husband went away upon a journey, after telling her that he expected her, before his return, to have not only learned to spin, but to have spun a hundred balls of thread. Quite downcast, she took a walk along the hillside, till she came to a big flat stone, and there she sat down and cried. By and by she heard a strain of fine music, coming as it were from underneath the stone, and, on turning it up, she saw a cave below, where there were sitting six wee ladies in green gowns, each one of them spinning on a little wheel, and singing:

"Little knows my dame at hame
  That Whippety Stourie is my name."

The lady walked into the cave, and was kindly asked by the wee bodies to take a chair and sit down, while they still continued their spinning. She observed that each one's mouth was twisted away to one side, but she did not venture to guess the reason. They asked why she looked so unhappy. She told them that she was expected by her husband to be a good spinner, when the plain truth was that she could not spin at all, and found herself quite unable for it, having been so delicately brought up. Neither was there any need for it, as her husband was a rich man.

"Oh, is that all?" said the little wifies, speaking out of their cheeks alike.

"Yes," said the lady, her heart like to burst with distress.

"We could easily quit ye of that trouble," said the wee women. "Just ask us all to dinner for the day when your husband is to come back. We'll then let you see how we'll manage him."

So the lady asked them all to dine with herself and her husband, on the day when he was to come back.

When the good man came home, he found the house so occupied with preparations for dinner, that he had no time to ask his wife about her thread, and, before ever he had once spoken to her on the subject, the company was announced at the hall door. The six fairy ladies all came in a coach-and-six, and were as fine as princesses, but still wore their gowns of green. The gentleman was very polite, and showed them up the stairs with a pair of wax candles in his hand. And so they all sat down to dinner, and conversation went on very

pleasantly, till at length the husband, becoming familiar with them, said:

"Ladies, if it be not an uncivil question, I should like to know how it happens that all your mouths are turned away to one side?"

"Oh," said each one at once, "it's with our constant spin-spin-spinning."

"Is that the case?" cried the gentleman. "Then, John, Tam, and Dick, make haste and burn every rock, and reel, and spinning-wheel in the house, for I'll not have my wife to spoil her bonnie face with spin-spin-spinning."

And so the lady lived happily with her good man all the rest of her days.

The Elves and the Shoemaker

By the Brothers Grimm

Once there was a shoemaker who worked hard from morn to night. The shoes he made were of the finest leather, but business was slow. One night he found he only had enough leather left for one more pair of shoes. With a heavy heart, he cut the leather carefully and left the pieces ready on his work bench to sew the next morning. He blew out the candle, and crossed the yard from his little shop into the house.

The next day the shoemaker was up early as usual. When he pulled back the shutters in the shop, you can imagine his surprise when he saw not pieces of leather ready to sew on the bench, but a fine pair of ladies' shoes with delicate pointed toes. The stitching was so fine you would think it had been done by mice. He put the shoes in the window of the shop, and before long a rich merchant came in and bought the shoes for his new wife, paying the poor shoemaker double the usual price. The shoemaker was delighted at this

turn in his fortunes, and bought enough leather to make two new pairs of shoes. Once again, he cut the leather, and left the pieces on his work bench to sew the next day.

The next day the shoemaker was up even earlier than usual. His wife came with him as he went into the shop, and pulled back the shutters.

"Oh husband," she gasped, for there on the bench stood two pairs of the finest shoes she had ever seen. There was a green pair with red heels, and a pair so shiny and black the shoemaker could see his face in them. He put the shoes in the window, and very quickly in came a poet who bought the green pair with red heels, and not far behind him there was a parson who bought the shiny black pair. And both paid him a great deal of money for the splendid shoes with stitching so fine you would think it had been done by mice.

This continued for many days. The shoemaker would buy new leather and leave the pieces cut ready on his bench at night, and when he came back in the morning there would be the most exquisite shoes. The shoemaker's reputation spread, and his shop was soon full of customers. Before long the shoemaker and his wife were no longer poor, but they still lived simply as they had little wish for the luxuries of life.

One day, the wife said, "Husband, I think we must see who has given us this good fortune so we may thank them."

The shoemaker agreed, so that night after laying out the cut leather pieces, he and his wife hid behind the door of the shop. As the town hall clock struck midnight, they heard a scampering of tiny feet and little voices, laughing. Two elves slid out from behind the skirting board and climbed

onto the bench where they were
soon hard at work,
stitching away
with tiny
stitches that
were so fine
they might
have been done
by mice. The elves

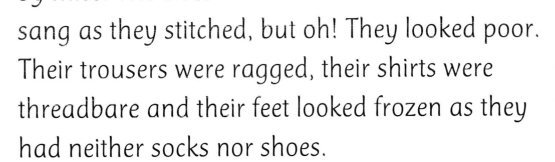

sang as they stitched, but oh! They looked poor.
Their trousers were ragged, their shirts were
threadbare and their feet looked frozen as they
had neither socks nor shoes.

Soon the leather was gone, and on the bench
stood more shoes. The elves slipped away.

The next day, the shoemaker took some green-
and-yellow leather and made two little pairs of
boots, yellow with green heels. The wife took some

cloth and made two little pairs of red trousers and two green jackets with silver buttons. She knitted two little pairs of socks. That night, they laid out the clothes and boots, and hid behind the shop door.

As the town hall clock struck midnight, the two elves slid out from behind the skirting board and climbed onto the bench. When they saw the gifts, they clapped their hands in delight, flung off their old rags and tried on their new clothes and the boots. They looked splendid. Then they slipped behind the skirting board, and the shoemaker and his wife never saw them again.

But once a year when the shoemaker opened the shop in the morning, on his bench he would find a pair of shoes with stitching so fine you would think it had been done by mice.

The Fairy Cure

By Patrick Kennedy

For nearly a year, Nora's daughter, Judy, had been in bed with a sore leg. There was nothing that anyone could do.

Nora was a midwife, and one night she was whisked away to a magnificent palace to help a lady about to have a child. In the hall she saw an old neighbour, who warned Nora not to take any refreshments or reward. She could, however, take a cure for a fairy disease.

She found the lady of the castle in a bed and in a short time she gave birth to a beautiful little girl. "I am so pleased with you," said the lady. "Please take as much gold, silver and jewels out of the next room as you can carry."

Out of curiosity, Nora stepped in and saw piles of gold and silver coins, and baskets of diamonds and pearls, lying about on every side, but she remembered her caution.

"I'm much obliged to you, my lady," said she, "but if I took jewels home, no one would ever call on me again to help his wife, and I'd be sitting and doing nothing but drinking tea. I'd be dead before a year'd gone by."

"Oh dear!" said the lady, "What an odd person you are! At any rate, sit down at that table, and help yourself to food and drink."

"I'm not hungry, thank you ma'am."

"Alas! Is there any way in which I can show you how grateful I am for your help and skill?"

"Indeed is there, ma'am. My girl, Jude, has had a sore leg for twelve months, an' I'm sure that the lord or yourself can make her as sound as a bell if you only say the word."

"Ask me anything but that."

"Oh, lady, dear, that's giving me everything but the thing I want."

"You don't know the offence your daughter gave to us, or you would not ask me to cure her. You know that all the fairy court enjoy their lives in the night only, and we frequently go through the country, and hold our feasts where the kitchen, and especially the hearth, is swept up clean. About a twelvemonth ago, myself and my ladies were passing your cabin, and one of the company liked the appearance of the neat thatch, and the

whitewashed walls, and the clean pavement outside the door, so much, that she persuaded us all to go in. We found the cheerful fire shining, the well swept hearth and floor, and the clean pewter and plates on the dresser, and the white table. We were so well pleased, that we sat down on the hearth, and laid our tea tray, and began to drink our tea as comfortably as could be."

"We were vexed enough when we saw your daughter come out of your bedroom, and make towards the fire. Her feet were clean, but one of them would cover two or three of us. On she came, and just as I was raising my cup of tea to my lips, down came the soft flat sole on it, and spilled the tea all over me. I was very much annoyed, and I caught the thing that came next to my hand, and hurled it at her. It was the tea pot, and the point of the spout is in her leg from that night till now."

"Oh, lady! The poor girl didn't know you were there!"

"Well, take this ointment, and rub it where you will *see* the purple mark, and I hope that your thoughts of me may be pleasant."

With that, Nora returned home, stripped the clothes off her daughter's leg, rubbed some of the stuff on it, and in a few seconds she saw the skin bursting, and a tiny spout of a tea-pot working itself out.

From then on, they took good care never to let their feet stray after bedtime, for fear of hurting any unseen visitors.